C000091950

DARK PARADISE

ROSA LIKSOM DARK PARADISE TRANSLATED BY

DAVID MCDUFF DALKEY ARCHIVE PRESS

Originally published in Finnish as *Tyhjän tien paratiisit*
by WSOY, Helsinki, Finland, 1989
Copyright © 1989 by Rosa Liksom and WSOY
Translation copyright © 2007 by David McDuff

First Dalkey Archive edition, 2007   All rights reserved

Partially funded by grants from the National Endowment for
the Arts, a federal agency, the Illinois Arts Council, a state
agency, and the University of Illinois, Urbana-Champaign

This work has been published thanks to the
Finnish Literature Information Center (FILI)

Dalkey Archive Press is a nonprofit organization whose mission
is to promote international cultural understanding and
provide a forum for dialogue for the literary arts

DALKEY ARCHIVE PRESS   University of Illinois
605 E. Springfield, MC-475, Champaign, IL 61820

www.dalkeyarchive.com

Design and composition by Quemadura
Printed on permanent/durable acid-free, recycled paper,
bound in the United States of America, and
distributed throughout North America and Europe

CONTENTS

DOMESTIC

AFTER THE FUNERAL SHE LOCKED HERSELF IN THE BEDROOM. For twelve days she didn't eat or drink or sleep. The sun rose and set, but she didn't notice. She felt like a stranger, and everything she saw and thought seemed completely disconnected. She didn't think back to the old days, but she could still detect her husband's smell in the sheets of the double bed. There had been moments when they were happy. When a baby, round and newly born, lay gurgling on the carpet on Sunday mornings; when her husband lay lazily beside her; when she sat, pretty and fragrant, in the front seat of the car on her way to work. It was all long ago, or maybe it had only just happened. Or maybe it was all just in her imagination.

She sat up naked in bed. She looked at herself in the bedroom mirror, which was fixed to the ceiling. She looked closely, but couldn't see anything. Not even her own face. She took a heavy vase from the floor and threw it at the mirror, which shattered into large and small pieces. The shards cut her all over.

Some of the wounds were deep—they gaped and spurted blood. The sheets were stained red, her body throbbed, and the blood smelled of something old and oppressive. She hopped down to the floor. The pieces of mirror cut into the soles of her feet, but she didn't feel anything. She danced feverishly from one end of the room to the other, humming a tune she didn't know. The white flowered wallpaper turned red, the blood gushed out over her breasts and thighs. When she stopped dancing and fell to the floor unconscious, the last drops of blood formed a puddle in her lap.

I'LL TAKE TWO HUNDRED. OR FORGET IT. LOOK, I'VE JUST SPENT sixteen days in jail, and then they kick me out in the middle of the fucking night. So I sit down and do some math: I don't have bus fare, don't have cab fare, and a private jet is pretty much out of the question. Here I am in the goddamn shit. I've got nothing. No Visa card, no money. They took everything, every fucking thing. The stiletto, the safety pins, the bottle-opener, the cigarettes. Not that any of that stuff matters, but they took my rubber stamp too. That thing was my most prized possession— you wouldn't believe what I went through to get it to work. Nine months tinkering with the damned thing, and now they've taken it. You have no idea how I froze up when that fucking cop pulled it out of my pocket and threw it in the garbage. A little while later the cleaning lady came along and took it away, who the hell knows where. It's the most depressing thing that's ever happened to me—my stamp and nine months' work straight down the toilet. A person gets nothing for nothing in this world. Life's worn me down. You'd think I'd committed some

5

horrible crime, some unforgivable sin, and this is my punishment. They kept me in that cell for sixteen days, they didn't even interrogate me, when really my only crime was that for once in my life I got something to work. That rubber stamp was my greatest achievement—it was perfect. It's not just anybody who can make something as perfect as that. Perfect—do you understand? *Perfect*. But then I lost it. Sixteen days. Although I wouldn't have given a shit about that if only I'd gotten the stamp back. It was my love, my wife, my mistress. And now I'm standing here with my ass to the Pasila police station and I'll be damned if I'll leave until they give it back. I'll go back to that fucking glass window and wage a one-man war. I'll sit there as stiff as a crowbar and just wait until they find my stamp and give it back to me, even if they have to bring it all the way from the garbage dump on the other side of town. I'll chain myself to a radiator and sit there until they beg for mercy and bring my stamp back, and if it's damaged, they'll fucking well replace it, even if they have to go to a doctor's office to get a new one. I'll be damned if I give in. Who gives up their most cherished possession without a fight? Not me—they'll have to kill me first. I'll charge in, chain myself to a radiator, and demand my stamp back. I'll call all the newspapers, they'll run front-page head-

lines about me and my one-man war against the whole goddamn Pasila police force. I'll show those cops who's got balls.
I'm no pussy—what's mine is mine. Because I know what it is
to love something, and they don't, they don't have the slightest
idea how much I love my stamp, they don't have a clue. They
don't know what real love is. Christ, all the shit I've been
through with that stamp. Sometimes we've been down, and
other times we've been up so high that no one could get higher,
not in Finland anyway. In America in the sixties, maybe, but not
here. Never—and now I'm all on my own, and damn it, I won't
survive without my stamp. I'll shoot anybody who tries to get in
my way. I want revenge on the shits that took it away from me.
I'll fucking well get a sawed-off shotgun and blow the head off
the Runeberg statue, I'll get my revenge. Oh, my stamp, without you I'll go right to hell. I'll just die here. I'll die right here,
and with my dying breath I'll whisper the most beautiful word
in the world. The word I engraved on my stamp, the word that's
kept me alive in this shitty world. *Valium*. And then that wonderful phrase: Mannerheim Street Surgery, K. Vesterinen. A
hundred thousand perfectly faked prescriptions, all for my own
personal use. Valium, my old friend, my strength, I am forever
yours.

DAD GOT ME AN APARTMENT IN EIRA—COST HIM AN EVEN MILLION
—after we'd had some little spats back in Haukilahti. Our problem was hygiene. There was dust everywhere. The shower was
a complete mess. I had to disinfect it every time I used it, and I
never used the toilet until I'd put a sterile covering on the seat.
Anyway, we were fighting about this all the time, so Dad finally
got me a place of my own. A nice apartment with high ceilings.
Completely modernized. I moved out and was really relieved to
think that now I wouldn't have to spend all day cleaning. But
when I'd been in the new apartment for a couple of days, it occurred to me that I knew nothing about the previous owner—
he could've been gay, for all I knew—so I bought some disin-
fectants and spent three weeks scrubbing the place down. I
went over every inch with a fine-tooth comb, until finally the
place was really clean, and I started to think about getting a job.
I spent a couple of days thinking about what I wanted to do, but
then I noticed that the window ledges were covered in thick

soot, no doubt all kinds of air pollutants had gotten in, and so there was nothing to do but stop thinking about jobs and start cleaning again. So there I was cleaning, and I didn't have time to do anything else. Luckily Dad brought me food from Stockmanns every day, so I didn't need to make the effort of going out on top of everything else. Stockmanns' stuff is okay with me, but Dad's visits turned out to be a problem. He's a businessman and flies all over the world, so you can imagine all the diseases he unknowingly carries around with him. Each time he showed up, I had to disinfect everything he'd touched. So the summer went by and I never once went out. How could I, when everything out there was so filthy and polluted? Then it was September and Mari came back from Greece. She came dressed all in white, because she knows how important cleanliness is to me. At first everything was okay, but then she wanted to kiss, and I felt nauseated thinking about all the diseases she must've picked up. I told her we could do that later, when she'd had a shower and disinfected herself. When she came out of the shower, I took her by the hand and kissed her, but then I remembered that you can get AIDS from French kissing, and I panicked. I asked if she'd been unfaithful, but she swore she hadn't. Eventually she went home, and left me a bottle of Greek wine. I poured it down the toilet, disinfected the bowl, and went to bed, but I couldn't sleep. I had to clean all the places that Mari had touched. I cleaned until five in the morning, and slept all the next day. Mari brought me some hot food from Stockmanns after work and said she wanted us to make love. Not on your life, I said, not with a woman who's just come back from Greece! I explained that we might reappraise the situation in a few months' time, and if she didn't show any symptoms of disease, then maybe then. Mari agreed, and was nice about going home. Luckily she'd only sat on three of my chairs, and cleaning them only took half the night. The autumn went by, and everything continued as before, Mari brought food and Dad came by now and then to check that everything was okay. No one said anything about a job, least of all me, because by then I realized that I'd never be able to cope with a job in addition to all that cleaning. And I couldn't imagine working in some dirty office breathing the same air as all those other people. At Christmas, Mari and I discussed sleeping together. I was almost convinced, but changed my mind at the last minute, just to be on the safe side. In the spring we got married, because Mari wanted it, and so did Dad. The pastor came to the apartment and married us there, and Dad gave me hand weights as a wedding present. After the wedding, I cleaned everywhere, then took up bodybuilding. Mari was thrilled when my muscles started to grow. She kept coming by once a week with the week's food. Luckily her visits grew shorter and shorter, and there was no more talk about sex. I trained and cleaned all day, and after a year I had these enormous muscles, like my biceps were almost bursting even before I flexed them. My thighs were like two icebergs from the North Pole. Mari didn't visit anymore. It was just as well, since cleaning up after her was hellish. I haven't seen anything of Mom since I moved away from Haukilakhti, but Dad's gotten a lot more sensible. Nowadays when he visits he has polyethylene bags on his shoes and a white coat over his clothes. He wears a sterile mask and a pair of disposable plastic gloves.

IT ALL STARTED SOME TIME BEFORE MY EIGHTH BIRTHDAY. I was lounging in an armchair in the parlor watching Mom make dinner in the kitchen. That was the first time the realization came to me. I got this terrible nauseous feeling, a flash of lightning cut right through my brain and Mom suddenly looked to me like some sort of mutant, a caricature of a human being. I know that's when it started, and the years have only made it clearer to me that even then, as a little kid, I was one-hundred-percent correct: I hate all women. I hate every woman I pass on the street, in the park, on the beach, or in the office. I get goose bumps when I have to look them in the eye or exchange some friendly words with them. I do those things, of course—through the years I've even gotten good at them. I can talk without effort, even with a smile, to women I don't know at all, but it doesn't get rid of the hatred and loathing I feel. I would gladly get rid of every woman on the face of the Earth. I'd like to establish a state for men only, a large region with strict borders, rich in natural resources, where everything is decided by the size of a man's cock. The bigger the cock, the greater the power. Women are disgusting creatures, and they're mentally deficient even from a scientific point of view. Our slimy cunts, bleeding orifices, gaping mouths, stinking armpits. Yes, they know the truth about us, and so I've been thinking about a new law that from next year onwards would make it legal to cut the throats of all female babies right there in the maternity hospital. In a hospital it could be done very hygienically and in the most natural way.

I've lived with my mother for eighteen years and it's always just been me and her. By the time I was born my father was already gone, and good riddance. I never missed him, and I wouldn't have had any use for him. I shared everything with my mother ever since I was small, and in my teenage years, when children don't generally get along with their parents, we got along even better than before. My mother's never had a job. She was always at home when I was little, and I liked that. Other children were hauled off to kindergartens or looked after by relatives, but I was always allowed to stay. She's been on welfare for at least the past eighteen years, they say she hasn't been right in the head since she was a kid, but I've never noticed anything like that. Well, I admit that she's a bit on the quiet side, shy, perhaps, and she's never been one for going out. Ever since I was little, I was the one who did the shopping and went down to the newsstand and bought the lottery tickets. We got along very well together. In the evenings we watched TV, sometimes we played Ludo, and there was at least one occasion when she tried to read me stories. She crocheted bedcovers, which she sold to gypsies, and she made a little spending money from it. She would give me the cash immediately and let me buy what I wanted. We lived on the sixth floor, and from there we had a wonderful view of the Malmi fire station. We used to try to guess when the sirens were about to go off and the red lights start flashing. Then we tried to guess where the fire was and how large, and the next day we'd check the newspaper to see which of us was closer. She was really sweet, a tiny little doll, blonde and fast on her feet, though not as slim as I would've liked. I always came straight home from school and never played outside with the other children— they didn't interest me. I've never liked any of that gang stuff. I'm a quiet person and have always preferred being at home. I got good grades in school, though I was bullied all the time. My mother consoled me at home and I didn't care about the kids at school. I was more mature than all of them put together, but even so I decided that I wasn't going to stay at school any longer than I had to. That was okay by Mom, so I got a job at the post office, and she was thrilled because a state job came with a pension. Everything went incredibly well. Then one evening when I came home from work, she had already gone to bed. I was a bit surprised, thought it a little odd for her to go to bed so early. For as long as I could remember, she'd never gone to bed before I got home. I thought I would just let her sleep, though, and I made up the sofa for myself. When I woke up the next morning she was still lying there, with all her clothes on, even her apron. I thought she must be sick so I went to the pharmacy and bought some Tylenol and some aspirin, in case it was flu. She didn't take the tablets even though I waved them at her. She went on sleeping in the same position and never said a word. Of course she was the quiet type, but this was unusual. I went to my job, in the afternoon I did some shopping, and then I cooked up a meal as best I could. I made some for Mom, too, but she didn't even touch it. I talked to her and after a week or two she began to answer in short sentences and asked me to wash her and give her a new nightgown. I said I would, though I was very uncomfortable seeing her naked. I didn't want to undress her,

15

but I had to. She had her eyes closed and a sort of pleasant smile on her face. I avoided looking straight at her. She was as heavy as a sack of cement, but I did it anyway, and then went off to work, expecting that she'd get better and life would return to normal. I wondered if I ought to call the doctor, but thought he'd probably take her to the hospital, and I wouldn't allow that. I wanted to look after Mom myself, and anyway she said she didn't want the doctor. I washed and changed her nightgown for her and learned how to do all the household chores. Then one Friday the building manager let himself in with his key and stood there looking around. He said the neighbors had been complaining about a peculiar smell. He said he'd come to check and see what we were up to. It occurred to me that I hadn't aired the place for months. I opened the window and told him that my mother was sick and so everything was a bit muddled. He glanced at the bed and went away, but when I came home the next night they'd gone and taken her away from me. I'd hardly had time to take stock of the situation when the building manager let himself in again, along with two policemen. I asked what was going on, but they wouldn't tell me. They asked me politely to accompany them to their car. Of course I went, because I thought they'd take me to her. Instead they drove me here, and I was taken to a ward. I still don't know what's going on. They're keeping me here, and I can't go to work, or even visit Mom in the other ward. We don't even get a room together. Everything is really in a mess and I can't ask her what it means.

WE GOT MARRIED ON THE FOURTEENTH OF NOVEMBER AND IT
was all over before the end of the month. For me it was a marriage that lasted exactly two weeks too long. I met him in Pampam where a group of us had gone for a beer after work. He
came in through the door and I thought *this guy is made for me*. At
the end of the night I went up to his table and told him to kiss
my ass. He liked that. We went back to my place, and after that
I couldn't get rid of him. Just one night together, but the creep
wouldn't go away! He glued himself to my bed. He was asleep
when I left for work and damn it if he wasn't still asleep with his
butt in the air when I got home. He didn't go to work, didn't go
out for groceries, didn't even empty the trash. I put up with it all
because I liked him a bit, in bed at least, when he wasn't sleeping. After a week he asked me to marry him and I agreed, because it was fucking November and it was freezing out, even in
Pampam. I thought, well now I'll have something to celebrate
with my friends from work. Doesn't really matter who I get mar-

ried to, it'll be okay. The wedding was held at the Savoy, I wore a white wedding dress, we got a few presents, drank ourselves silly, and everyone had a roaring great time. Then came the day after, and the guy did crosswords in bed, and stank. I even put up with that, but when we'd been married a week he started to whine about what an unhappy childhood he'd had and what a terrible adolescence, and how nobody cared about him and he had nothing to live for. Christ, I listened to him all week, every night the same whining, and there I was, thinking at last I'd found a real man! So, after the first week of the marriage I was a nervous wreck, and started to wonder what the hell I was doing with a guy who just lay in bed sniveling all the time. The second week he got even worse, started blubbering about some grandmother dying twenty years ago. I told him he could just go to hell. He showed me his wedding ring. I threw mine out the window, but he didn't budge. I tried to drag him out to the stairs, but I couldn't move him. I called the cops and told them to take the damn guy away. The cops looked at me and then at the guy, and then they left. So I got out the fillet knife and stabbed him. He didn't even put up a fight, just croaked right there in the only bed I had. I called Hesperia Hospital and told the shrinks my husband had committed suicide by stabbing himself in the heart, and then went out to see a friend from work. She calmed me down, saying that things like that happen sometimes. We drank some coffee and in the morning we went to work. Next day I got a call from the police station, asking for more details. I told them everything and said I'd been on the toilet reading the newspaper when the guy just killed himself. They believed it all, and the girls at work thought I'd absolutely done the right thing. It was his own fault for lying there and whining and telling me all that bullshit. Damn it, I need a real man, someone who's in control, who can pay the rent and keep the refrigerator stocked. I mean, the man has responsibilities too, when you live together.

WHEN IT WAS PAST THREE IN THE MORNING, THE MAN TOOK A pistol from the drawer of the bedside table and loaded it. The man had black bags under his eyes from weeks of staying awake nights, and the wrinkles on his forehead and at the corners of his eyes had become deep furrows. The misty glow of a lamppost shone from the street below, revealing that the other half of the large double bed was empty. His wife had left him several years ago, moved back home with her aging mother on the other side of town. The man looked at the empty street outside. Palm trees, green springtime grass, a stray cat on the hood of a car. He aimed at the cat through the window, then lowered the weapon again. Five large rooms with plenty of space, Persian carpets and arrangements of fresh flowers. The man cast a glance at the door, as though afraid that someone might come in. It was a ridiculous thought; his son hadn't been in the bedroom since the man's wife had left him. The man looked back at the street, but the cat was gone. His mind should have been clear, focused, but stories from his childhood, about people dying young and coming back as tormented ghosts, distracted him for a moment. A heavy feeling of guilt settled on him. After a moment, he managed to shake it off. He opened the bedroom door and walked resolutely through the living room, the dining room, the library. He stopped at the end of the hall and felt like he was ready to do it. He had no one else in the world but his son. In all his long life he couldn't remember a single moment of pleasure. Even in the marriage bed, an angel had sat on his shoulder, tallying up all the sins committed from the fall of mankind onward. He went quietly up to the door of his son's room and carefully opened it. He felt a violent spasm of nausea. His son was fast asleep, and next to him lay a naked woman. Cold shivers ran down the man's back and then over his entire body. He looked at the woman's large breasts and painted lips and felt even more miserable than before at the sight of these people sinning in their sleep. He raised his arm and took aim. He slowly pressed the trigger and felt an immense sense of triumph—only after losing everything would he emerge in his own eyes as the victor. Then he lowered his arm and the pistol fell to the floor. He was trembling. His eyes grew wide with horror and he closed the door again. He started to cry. He wiped his tears away, swallowed his sobbing, went to his bedroom, put the pistol away in the nightstand drawer, and covered his head with a pillow.

ON SATURDAY MORNING I SET OUT FOR THE STORE CARRYING
a plastic bag full of empty bottles. I got to the store, turned in
the bottles, picked up new ones, and paid at the checkout
counter in the usual way. The sun was shining pleasantly and I
started off towards home. I passed the telephone booth that
stands on the edge of the football field, where it's always stood,
and then called a taxi. Before long I was sitting in the back seat,
telling the driver to take me to the center of town. I don't know
what came over me, but the next thing I knew I was sitting in a
bar with my sixth beer in front of me, looking for young women.
I walked over to the next table and found one to take home. She
was under twenty, with a big mouth and a tight ass. We took my
bottle with us and went back to her place. She lived in a squat
little house, and her parents were away at their summer cottage.
First we drank beers and then we fucked for an hour or two and
then we went back to the bar. A couple of days went by like that,
with some friends joining in, although the girl got lost some-

where on the first night. I don't know what happened to her. I spent the whole of Tuesday drinking with my buddies, Veli and Mauno. On Wednesday I went to the Black Kettle to have a morning beer for my awful hangover when Veli's wife showed up and told me to come with her. She said Veli and Mauno had gone and bought a bottle of Koskenkorva and they were drinking like pigs. Well, I said, I sure as hell wasn't going to run off with a friend's wife. She insisted. I asked Veli for his advice. Veli said fuck it, she's okay. The woman called a taxi and we went to their place. She immediately took off all her clothes and made me do the same, though I was a little reluctant at first. She was a complete nutcase, wouldn't let me out of the place for three days. We drank vodka and Pommac and probably spent some time in the sauna. She was desperate for a fuck—I had no choice. No man wants a woman thinking he can't perform, after all—that kind of news spreads like wildfire in a little town like this. If you say no even once, you'll never get a woman again, your reputation is ruined. I managed, but it was rough. Then Veli came home in a taxi, the bastard. It must have been Saturday morning. I told him he could keep his wife, I was going home. He realized right away what I'd been doing with her. I felt really sick, but I decided to walk home on my own two legs, to wake me up a bit before I had to face my own wife. I must have walked about twenty kilometers, and got home just before the six o'clock news.

"Where have you been?" screamed my wife, with the kids wrapped around her legs.

"I've been out drinking with the boys, you know that without having to ask," I said, and went to bed. She followed me in, quick as lightning, and kept shouting. I fell asleep and woke up now and then because of all her wailing, weeping, and shrieking. Then she quieted down all at once, as though someone had stuck a knife in her. She fell down beside me on the bed and started to grope me.

"Don't even try, I'm completely exhausted," I told her with a tremor in my voice. She pretended not to hear me. She undid my fly and stuck her hand in my pants and demanded that I fuck her too now, since all the whores in town had had their chance. I begged her to let me sleep for a couple of hours first, but the woman wouldn't hear of it and threw herself on top of me. I had no alternative. It was like burning in hellfire. A man can get sucked dry that way—but I fucked her and then she left me in peace and I was able to sleep till the next morning.

I'M A SIXTH-GENERATION NATIONALIST, AND PROUD OF IT. I've made it my mission to lead the country forward, to promote its traditions and ideologies, and I intend to do so at every opportunity. At school I tried to explain to my class that one day those goddamn Russians are going to come and stain red our blue-and-white flag, but something must be wrong with them, because they didn't pay attention. It's not that they were actually against me—it's just that they can't get it into their thick heads that the fatherland has to be defended at all times from the Russians. All the boys in my class are already planning to join the army as volunteers, but that isn't enough, for God's sake. Soldiers need to understand what our fatherland is— what the blue-and-white flag our forefathers gave their lives for really means. It's not enough to go around in a gray uniform thinking that because you know how to shoot, you're already doing your part. Certainly every young Finnish man has to learn to shoot straight—if we don't shoot straight, the goddamn

27

Russians will overwhelm us through their numbers alone! They'll keep us under their yoke till the end of history if we don't take destiny into our own hands and attack them first, send their blood spurting! At school I've impressed on the teachers that it's not enough for them to talk and talk about the fatherland to the students; I think teachers need to teach their students to love this country with all their hearts and souls. Schoolchildren have to learn to respect the purity and prosperity of this country, protect it against unclean blood and all the other, uncivilized peoples who are trying to force their way into our land—this land which thanks to us has become one of the most advanced and civilized in the world! I explain it to them but they just go on listening to disco music and talking about soap operas and women's magazines. The boys just shoot for fun on hunting trips and run after girls in between. None of them have any respect for anything. From when I was a little kid, my dad taught me the meaning of national defense, of military power, what it means to have a country of one's own. I grew up with a real affection for the fatherland, not like those other kids. I understand these things, and am far wiser and more far-sighted than any of the teachers. Together with Dad I've gone through all of Finland's wars ten times. I know the day-to-day positions of the front lines during the Continuation War and understand how events escalated from week to week. I know about all the most modern weapons and can take apart and re-assemble rifles and handguns. I know all the military ranks in all the armies of the world by heart, and know how to make a nuclear bomb and how to defuse an ordinary bomb or hand grenade. Dad taught me everything from the basics up, and when he turned forty and I was only eleven, I was already able to dismantle a machine gun and hit a moving target right in the head. Everyone who came to his birthday party saw it and was really amazed. I always went along with Dad to the training camp before I started school, and just recently during the Christmas holidays I was with him at the training camp over at Salla. I was a far better shot than either the recruits or the junior officers. I usually ski a little there with Dad, he lets me shoot his gun, and then together we talk over different kinds of military strategies. I want to learn how to run a war, because one day people like me will be needed and I don't think I'll be happy just clearing mines. I want to be a leader, I want to be in the nerve center, leading the Finns to victory and seeing that the Russians are killed down to the last man. Dad taught me that girls have to be able to do all the same jobs as boys, and I always have, and much more besides. With Dad I even wrote a letter to the president of the Republic, that insect, to ask that I be allowed to join the army as a volunteer under special dispensation when I'm seventeen. I've always dreamed of a military career; I want to be a professional soldier. First I'll join the Finnish Army, then I'll go to Germany for military training, and after that I'll become a mercenary and go and shoot Reds in Nicaragua. I plan to be such a good shot that no one will have seen anything like it in Finland since Mannerheim. I respect and admire Mannerheim above anyone else, he was a real man, with real backbone. I want to be a man like that and nothing will stop me. Not the Finnish laws that say I was born female, no, nothing. If that insect won't take me into the armed forces next year on a special dispensation, then I'll give up school and go to Chile. I refuse to bow to Finnish law. Dad promised to arrange the documents and pay for it all because he wants me to be a bright star in the annals of Finnish military history.

IN THE MORNING I GET UP AND MAKE COFFEE. I HAVEN'T GIVEN
up coffee, even though they're always talking about how it's the
root of all evil and so on. I make coffee, yes, very black and
strong. It does me good and then I take a shower. I sweat so hor-
ribly during the night lately that I'd smell all day if I didn't
shower first thing. I wash my armpits, then my ass, and then my
feet. I always like to be clean. I even put powder and eau-de-
cologne on my stomach. By eight o'clock I turn on the radio. I
eat some salami and spread butter on several slices of healthy
rye bread. They taste good. At nine I go out and take Musti to
Paavola, who looks after him. He always gets looked after in the
mornings—he can't be left at home alone. He's not used to me
being away from home all the time, and now that there's a new
regime I have to think of the dog, too, not just of myself. At ten
I go to the Weight Watchers meeting. There they weigh me and
give me advice and then I gossip with the ladies for a few hours
and talk about everything that happened the day before. Actu-

ally, I have meetings every day—I belong to five different groups and pay five different membership fees, but that's okay. Nowadays you really have to pay for your hobbies. What they say is true, you don't get anything for nothing, and anyway I just pay so I can gossip. Otherwise I'd be very lonely. Down there at the Weight Watchers meetings we have very light meals, sip energy drinks, and get advice. No one gives a damn about the advice, not even the counselors. We just nod and talk about our problems. The time really flies, and we enjoy ourselves. Those drinks and salads make you fart, they don't fill you up or quench your thirst, but you can get through those meetings if you eat a good breakfast before you leave home. Then when we come out of Weight Watchers, all of us ladies go to the taxi drivers' bar. There we all order apple-jam doughnuts and big glasses of milk. We chat a bit more and the taxi drivers tease us. They're nice guys who like to shoot their mouths off, we sometimes play lotto with them. After the bar I usually go and play bingo, and the ladies go wherever it is they go. I have fun with Jussi Nieminen and Veikko Kaartinen till about two or three and then I have to go and get Musti. Paavola has a job as a janitor for an insurance company, so I have to go and fetch Musti no matter how well I'm doing at bingo. We stop off at the store on the way home and I buy a liver casserole for Musti and a bologna ring for myself. I eat it over the course of the evening. I eat it straight from the fridge, cut up into small pieces, and I don't bother putting mustard on it. Bologna rings are good, and they satisfy your hunger better than that crap they give you at Weight Watchers. Musti and I watch TV, I file the hard skin off my feet, and Musti lies and gnaws at a leg of the sofa. We have a good time. After the news is over we settle down in the kitchen and eat smoked salmon sandwiches and drink sour milk. Smoked salmon is so cheap nowadays that even I can afford it. It's not real salmon, but anyway it's red, and salty enough. Then we go to bed together, and wait for a new day.

I WAS THIRTY-SIX WHEN I WENT TO SERVE MY SENTENCE UP there in Hämenlinna. I stuffed my duffel bag full of thick flannel underwear so I wouldn't freeze to death. I'd more or less prepared myself for the bedrooms there to be incredibly damp, cold, and horrible, but they weren't cold at all. The rooms are okay, actually—better than I had at home at the time. I'd really imagined it would be a fucking labor camp with guards that whipped you and shouted. But they weren't like that; they were all quiet types who kept to themselves. The work was just a little bit of this and and a little bit of that, and nobody threatened you if you sat on the john a bit longer than usual, like they do in factories. Actually, looking back on it, I'd say it was better working there than in a factory. In a factory you have a goddamn bourgeois pig riding your ass all day, and if you take a break once too often the pig fires you on the spot. Up there in Hämenlinna you could have a cigarette, or even two, and the guards just yawned at you. And I had some particularly lazy guards or guardettes or whatever they were called. One of them had this great big round belly, and when she had to climb a few stairs she'd puff and pant like a walrus. Another one had dropped out of college and gone to work in the prison instead. My God she looked depressed, like she was going to quit any day now. The other women said that this woman really planned to finish school, get her degree and all that. But I don't believe it. She was there when I arrived, and she'll be there until she dies— mark my words. She's probably never even opened a book, was just trying to come off as smart. I was there in jail for nine years. You could get parole, but I never bothered trying. Where would I have gone? There was hot food on the table every day, and on Sundays we were allowed to sleep until eight. So, no, I didn't apply for parole, though they tried to throw me out by force once. I told them I wasn't going anywhere and that they couldn't make me. They didn't understand, but I was too shy to explain that it was a matter of principle. I'd decided long before anything happened that I was going to serve out whatever sentence I got, every single day of it, and even if they tried to chuck me out only halfway through, I wouldn't go. And I stuck to that. I was there for exactly nine years, that makes 3,285 days plus two leap-year days, and I was so stubborn that I waited at the door for exactly one hour and five minutes before I would agree to step through. I remember that the guy who was guarding that door looked at me as though I was a complete idiot, but I just sat there and let the guy stare. Then my time was served, though, and I've never given it a moment's thought since. I've made my restitution to the state and to my conscience, and since that day they closed the door behind me, I've lived a new life. I started everything over from scratch. I was forty-five then, and in good shape. I was given a rail ticket to my home village and I took the first train that morning. Nothing much had changed there in nine years. I trudged up to my old house, but it was damn cold and the windows were broken. It was in early spring when I was released, and I thought, well, this will do for the summer. I nailed up planks over the windows and lit the kitchen stove. I'm a woman who knows how to cope with life. I tore down the outhouse and used it as firewood. It's true that the villagers were a bit surprised. But nobody came to see who'd lit the stove. They knew enough to keep their distance. The kitchen was a wreck, everything turned inside out. Some kids had gotten in and made a mess—they'd tried to burn the rocking chair and smashed all my dishes. I cleared the junk away. I chopped firewood and cleaned, and pretty soon it wasn't so bad. The first night I slept in the hayshed—there was just enough hay in there to make it bearable. From time to time I went inside and put more wood in the stove. Next morning the kitchen was warm. I could unbutton my thermal underwear and sit down. Then gradually spring arrived. By then I'd moved the windowpanes of the cowshed to the kitchen and my house was just like a real home again. Of course, the villagers still wouldn't come to visit. I couldn't get any work, and had barely enough to buy food. I got checks from the social security office when they wouldn't take me back at the goddamn factory. Then when summer was over and I'd sold all the berries I'd picked, I thought: there's no way in hell this is going to work out. I'd go crazy unless I could talk to someone. Up in Hämenlinna there were always people around chatting, but in my village no one would even say hello to me. I went to the social security office and told the woman there to get me a ticket south, and she did. I set the house on fire and left. It felt pretty damn good to let it burn. I hopped off the train in Tampere and marched into the office of a cleaning service. I told a guy in a suit—he was probably the boss—to give a good woman a job. And he did. I went to a night hostel for women and stayed there for months, cleaning. Cleaning was something I was always good at, and I've never been afraid of

hard work. Then when winter came along I got a little place behind the railway station, and I lived there for nearly three years.
I cleaned and saved and put my affairs in order. I've gotten along
really well here in Tampere. I've always been treated like a human being, and the other workers and my neighbors talk to me
normally and don't know a thing about me. They don't know
and they don't need to know that things were once so bad for me
that I killed a man—me, this slim little thing. I went on cleaning for that company for so long that last year I retired on a pension. I cleaned and lived like a human being for twenty years.
Then I was turned out of my house, and I got one of those one-
room apartments from the council. They didn't have a choice.
After all, I couldn't live in a snowdrift. Plus my boss probably
pulled a string or two. I was the best cleaner in the whole company, and he knew it. He probably called the city fathers and
told them, Give this woman an apartment! Or maybe he didn't,
who the hell knows. I got this place, though, and I've made it really nice. I like being here on a pension, and now that I've got a
cat, well, the time just flies by. I have a sofa and armchairs, a
portable TV and a radio. I have everything I want and more.
Plastic flowers and glass horses and God knows how many lace

tablecloths. And no one even remembers that I was once in Hä-menlinna prison and that I once stabbed that fucking pig in the belly with a knife. Who wants to remember things like that when you have a place like this and time to make yourself look nice and go out dancing?

EVERY DAY I EAT AT LEAST TWO BARS OF MARABOU CHOCOLATE. Really. For breakfast I eat eight squares of milk Marabou, one Mars bar, and two Snickers. Or else I eat half a bar of Marabou and two Snickers. By the middle of the day I've already eaten a whole bar of Marabou, even though I try to control myself. I go in to see the boss and tell him that I have to go down to the snack bar and buy a Fazer's whole-nut bar or two. And then I go into the smoking room and have a few cigarettes and then eat a bar while I chat with the other ladies in the office for a bit. I usually offer them a little and sometimes they take a piece. Of course they're appalled at me eating chocolate in the middle of the day, but I just tell them that there has to be some enjoyment in a widow's life. And then I go back into the office again, work like crazy until five and then take the bus home. I get off at the stop with Siva and we go in and buy slices of Siva's favorite cake. It's one of those all-chocolate ones, nice and soft, with crunchy stuff on top. I buy one slice and usually also a couple of those really big chocolate bars, and a liter of milk. Those really big bars are actually meant for baking, but they're incredibly good, harder than Marabou and the squares are three times the size. Then I walk home and my daughter is back, she'll have had three mugs of cocoa and a package of chocolate biscuits. She eats chocolate too, and biscuits, and potato chips. I've hardly had time to get the door open when she's shouting for chocolate. But she has to wait until I've taken off my coat and sat down in front of the TV. Then I give her one of the bars and take the other for myself. We watch TV, eat chocolate, and occasionally I have a cigarette. I only smoke ten a night, that's something I've agreed to with my daughter. She hasn't started yet, but she says she's thinking about it. Then we'll smoke together. Well, it's better than smoking on your own. I get along with my daughter really well. The only thing is that she's a teenager and has an awful lot of pimples. In the paper they say that chocolate only makes pimples worse, but if you ask me that's nonsense. They don't know anything about it, they just want to deny young people their only joy in life. After the news I make coffee and we eat Siva's favorite cake, and then it's time for bed. I usually buy those big bars for the morning, so we don't have to run down to the store before I leave for work, and anyway at that hour it's still closed. My daughter eats and drinks her own stuff, and I have mine after she's gone to school. Sometimes we go on choco-

41

late-buying trips to Haparanda over in Sweden. We buy boxfuls of cheap Marabou and smuggle them through Customs to Finland. Over there you can get eleven different kinds of Marabou. They have six more than we have here. I drive and my daughter sits next to me. We stow the chocolate under the back seat and we've never once been stopped by Customs. Of course this is nothing compared to when my husband was alive. Back then we had a card from one of those wholesale companies and we used it to buy mountains of candy, and the most expensive kinds, too. When my husband died, that was the end of the expensive stuff. We don't have enough money for that now, we have to make do with chocolate bars and Snickers. I suppose you could say that we eat about half a kilo of chocolate a day, and that's not counting Siva's cake. It certainly is a lot, but I'm not fat. I don't put on weight, and neither does my daughter. We eat nothing but chocolate, and we're in good shape. Once I asked my doctor why we have such an appetite for chocolate and he said it was psychological, because I was alone. I can't really believe that, because my husband and I always used to eat chocolate. We had exactly the same taste in chocolate, and we smoked the same brand of cigarettes.

THE WOMAN'S LACE BLOUSE IS SHINING WHITE. HER BLACK curly hair lies in neat waves, and her heavy earrings sway as she chews on her greasy chicken leg in the Viking Lines cafeteria. The woman gives me a quick but sharp look and points to an empty chair at the end of the table.

"My husband was shot in the center of Ahtari three years ago, shot with a sawed-off shotgun at such close range that his whole head was sprayed against the kitchen wall."

The woman bites into a large piece of breast, chews quickly, and wipes the grease from the corners of her mouth with the back of her hand.

"It was a lot of work cleaning up the mess. You have no idea how hard it is to get blood and that half-dried brain stuff off. My mother and I scrubbed for three days with soda and a scrubbing brush before we got the kitchen even halfway clean. Though there are still some big stains left over on the cupboard walls.

Imagine—after three years! Human blood is really difficult to get out."

The woman slurps milk from a carton, digs around in her molars with her little finger, and then looks me straight in the eye.

"I became a widow at twenty-three. I was carrying his child then and it was really a difficult time. The baby was kicking in my belly and I still had to clean up my husband's brains. I mean, they could have killed him with a knife, like they used to do in the old days. That would have been tidier. Corpses were prettier in the old days, too. For example, my uncle was knifed when he was twenty-five with a clean stab straight to the heart. In the coffin he had a really contented smile on his face. But we'll never know about the expression on my husband's face, since his whole head and half of his ribcage got turned into hamburger."

The woman gathers the gnawed chicken bones into a large pile on the edge of her plate and gives out a loud belch.

THEY'LL COME TOWARDS THE END OF THE WEEK, ALL FIVE REGI-
ments of them, and they'll take over this wilderness. It'll bring
some life to our neck of the woods. They say they'll have big
tanks with them, helicopters, and probably nuclear weapons,
too. So we'll get a look at the very latest military equipment. It
was different when I was a kid, just a rifle in your hand and wet
rags on your feet. War is easy nowadays, it's all done by com-
puters, and the soldiers don't need to lift a finger. When I was a
kid, war was a rough business, the sweat and the shit just flew.
Nowadays the soldiers use perfume and put Brill cream in their
hair. So the world's moved on and that's just as well. If nowadays war is less messy, that can only be a good thing. I'm not
crazy enough to want the old days back again. Not on your life
—they were bad old days, and everything is better now.

45

My wife and I have developed a real interest in national defense ever since they started to talk about this war, it must be a
couple of years ago now. We've done a great deal of talking

about this subject, and what it was like during the Winter War and the Continuation War. Revisiting our memories.

And now it will be a real pleasure to see all those fine young men when they get here. They'll liven the place up and put some life into it. We live in a kind of stupor, but soon strong, healthy young men will arrive here from Helsinki. All that military activity will bring us together and create a real patriotic spirit. While the tanks are churning up the fields and the bombs are falling behind the sauna, we'll have something to look at and talk about. It's welcome, and it's what we've been longing for. Now our village will get a name for itself and who knows, maybe some of the young fellows will come and live here after the war. And then the folks down south will remember that our town's name still has a place on the world map.

MY HUSBAND DIED IN THIS BED, HE JUST SLUMPED AGAINST the wall without saying a word. He died so suddenly that I didn't have time to do anything. We'd been in the sauna and when we came back into the house again he complained about his chest and said he had a pain in it. I tried to get him to lie down, but he never listened to what I said. He just kept walking around, and he looked terrible. I noticed that, I was keeping an eye on him. I pretended to be watching a sports show on TV before going to bed. After a bit, he came to bed too, and then he was dead. He didn't even have time to pray, to have his sins forgiven, he went Godless to his grave, although I told the priest that he'd said he was sorry for his sins and had called on God at the end. I couldn't bring myself to call for a taxi so late at night to take him to the church, so I fell asleep beside him like I usually did, and only made the call after I'd had my morning coffee. The taxi driver arrived after the school run, put my husband's corpse in the back seat, and then drove it to the church, or probably straight to the morgue. I made sure it was buried quickly, and I didn't bother with much of a funeral. Me and my husband didn't have much to do with other people. We kept to ourselves and it was best that way. We didn't run around the village and we didn't keep the coffeepot warm for strangers. We were able to live in peace, because it's a long way from the village to our place, and nowadays people are so lazy that they can't manage to walk more than a meter on their own. He was buried in the second half of the winter, and I thought that everything would go on like before, but sure enough things changed. I started coughing, and the cough just got worse and worse. I couldn't sleep in anymore, because as soon as I went to bed it started, and it was bad. I kept the radio on loud from morning to night and tried to stop coughing. Of course I know that it's not a good sign if you're coughing all the time and can't get any sleep. I started taking my husband's pills. I don't know what they were but at least I could sleep again. I slept as sweet as a baby, although as soon as I woke, the phlegm would come up from my throat in bucketfuls. I only got up to put more wood in the stove and make broth. Then it was summer, and since I didn't need to heat the place I just lay in bed and drank sour milk and swallowed pills by the handful. My husband had stuffed the medicine cabinet full of them, since over the years the doctor had prescribed thousands of them for him, but he'd never wanted to take them. Well, I took them all, and slept like a log. By the autumn I was full of phlegm up to here and the trouble was that I couldn't manage to get to the medicine cabinet anymore. What else could you expect, since I'd been living on nothing but pills and sour milk for months. I don't know what I was thinking. I guess I just wanted to slip down into the grave and lie next to him again. That's probably how I saw it, and I didn't care about anything, never did any housework or anything at all. I just lay there, listened to the radio and the TV at the same time, waiting for death and coughing blood. But then one day that damned taxi driver came to the door and knocked. I was convinced it was the angel of death who'd come to collect me, but no, goddamn it, it was the taxi driver, and he dragged me out to his car. He took me to the health center and right away they put me into the clinic and started to examine me. And of course they found a thousand and one things wrong. Then they started giving me more pills, and yelled at me for not looking after myself. They even said I'd been on the verge of dying. I was that weak—I was practically nothing but skin and bone. And they yelled at me for peeing in my pants and lying in my own shit for months. I mean, there was nothing I could say. I don't even understand myself how it happened. That it all went so wrong. Anyway, I lay in the hospital for months and they fed me through a funny kind of tube and hooked me up to all kinds of machines. I put a little flesh back on my bones and started to get better. I'm in really good shape now that they've sent me home. They send a woman from the council to clean for me and bring me food. The nurse always comes when I need her, so they're looking after me. And now I understand why they keep an eye on poor old ladies like me. The real reason is that the council wants my house—but they'll wait in vain. I've left everything to my husband and he's left everything to me. When I die, my husband will inherit it all. So then they'll just have to bury the house with us in the grave-yard.

THERE WE SAT, ALL THREE OF US, WITH OUR WRISTS IN BAN-
dages, at a panoramic window in Lapinlahti Hospital, looking
out at the damp, spring-green, swaying landscape of midwin-
ter. Runis had the thickest bandages, but blood had seeped
through them only this morning. He was the one who'd been
cut deepest, of course, since he was never one for leaving things
half-done. A pathetic kind of perfectionist. Topis's face was
chalk-white, and there were thick reddish rings under his eyes.
He looked really bad. His eyes moved in slow motion across the
boring landscape. When they reached me, he began to smile his
Topis smile, I smiled back—I wasn't in any hurry. I'd cut open
one wrist, but had only scratched the other a bit, just for the sake
of appearances, really. It's not very often that I go all the way, so
to speak. Topis was trying to catch Runis's eye, and when he
succeeded, Runis laughed out loud, and wondered if maybe it
was time we got going. I checked to see that the hallway was
empty. A couple of crazies were sprinting along the wall to the
telephone booth and back, but we didn't pay any attention to

them. In my room I put on my clothes, then tore off the bandages and walked out through the main entrance. The woman at the reception desk watched me go with the same look of sullen disgust as she had when I arrived. Runis came next, and Topis last. We waited outside the gate under an old birch tree. Topis was making these wild grimaces, as though he was trying to keep himself from screaming. He'd left the bandage on his left hand, while both of Runis's wrists were still bound up. It was okay. We walked side by side along the park boulevard and stepped aside as a white taxi approached us. The world seemed familiar, the same as it had been the week before. We went to the Shell station on Leppasuo, had coffee, and then took the bus. We got off at Kontula and walked through the shopping center to Vesala. To Runis's place, like we usually did. The kitchen table was exactly as we'd left it, and the puddles of blood from the week before had congealed on the floor. Topis looked at me and winked. Runis was already at the sink, looking for the carving knife. I took it from him and could see from Topis's expression that he was ready. I cut first, as usual. A small surface wound. Then Topis immediately cut a deep wound in his right arm, yanked the bandage off his left one, and gave Runis the knife. Runis grinned, pulled off both bandages and made deep cuts in each artery.

IN THE DREAM THERE WERE WHITE FLOWERS EVERYWHERE. It was a bright Sunday in July and very quiet. I wondered at the number of flowers, at the strange, oppressive atmosphere and the sun's burning brightness, wondered where the garlands of flowers were from and who they were for. Then I was startled, and moved away from the window, went to a corner of the room, realizing that I was the one who was being honored in such a peculiar way. But where were all the people, where were the villagers, the children, the cats and dogs running around? Where were the festive tables, the white tablecloths, and the coffee service? I touched my face, but couldn't find it. I touched my body, my feet, my elbows, but couldn't feel anything. I looked down at my lap, and saw only emptiness. I was scared. I was afraid of being alone, that sense of nothingness, like being dead. Then there was a knock at the door. My uncle from Laa-jasalo entered in a long black coat, followed by my grandmother and grandfather and forestry officer Mattila—who was killed in the Continuation War—and his fiancée Maria. I was afraid of them and tried to hide behind the fireplace, behind the bathroom cabinet, and under a table. But they came after me, stretching out their pale hands. Maria's eyes were gentle, just as they had been before the war, grandmother sang softly to herself as she'd done when I was a child and watched her secretly through the crack in the bedroom door. They caught hold of me, took me away, put me in a coffin. Only then did I realize that I was dead.

I lay in bed next to Juhani, drenched in sweat from head to toe. Cautiously, I turned over and raised the quilt to let the cold air of the bedroom dry my sweat, and then lay awake until the morning. The morning was thick, misty, and murky. I walked through the village to school in order to sweep away the snow that had fallen during the night, and I felt as though my head was wrapped in cotton wool. I felt terrible all that winter. I couldn't get any sleep, and when I did sleep, I woke up earlier each time. Juhani didn't notice anything, explained my problems away as always, and fell into his drowsy, healthy sleep. In the spring, when the lake was freed from its thick shackles of ice, I realized what the dream had meant and decided to start the preparations. I made an appointment with the hairdresser in the village, something I hadn't done since my youngest was born. I had my hair curled and dyed it red, and had it cut so that it fit the shape of my face. When I got home, Juhani pulled me into his arms for the first time in two months. The next day I started my diet. I decided to have only water and crispbread with a little dried meat for supper. One evening, when the children were asleep, Juhani asked me reluctantly what was going on, since I was getting prettier and prettier with each day that passed. He suspected that I had slept with Lasse Nuuttinen, or was at least in love with him, but I assured him this was impossible. Why now suddenly, after fifteen years of marriage, would I decide to be unfaithful? I tried to explain that it's good for a woman to get slimmer and make herself look nice. At the beginning of June I made an appointment with the dentist to get some false teeth. Juhani protested, wondering why I wanted them. I said that nice teeth make you look a lot younger, and Juhani gave in. He had no alternative, since I was planning to pay for them with the money from the milk account. The milk account was in my name, and when it came to it, only I had the right to use it. So the teeth were made. I went to the village several times, the teeth were tested and measured, moulds were cast, and the filing was done. Juhani again suspected that I had some man in the village, but I didn't know anyone there, and

55

anyway, everyone in the village had always kept far away from me. I'd been an ugly, fat, and smelly peasant woman from the backwoods. August arrived. The summer had been unusually hot and fine, the grass in the meadows and the flowers by the sides of the ditches grew so that you could hear them rustling. We got more fish from the lake than we could eat, and all the signs pointed to a plentiful autumn. The frost hadn't disturbed the berry flowers. September came, and I looked twenty years younger—all the villagers were amazed when they saw me. The men of the village began to visit us more often and stayed longer. I noticed how they looked at me with lust. At night, Juhani would accuse me, and say it would be better if I were fat and ugly again. I put up with it—it all went in one ear and out the other.

In the first week of September, just before the lingonberry harvest, I went to buy new clothes for myself. Trousers, a jacket, shiny shoes, a silk blouse. When I came home, Juhani started swearing, asking me if I'd been whoring myself to rich men in town. I told him I'd paid for it all with the money from the blueberries. I was almost ready. After taking a sauna, I manicured my nails, rubbed my skin with cream for wrinkles, painted my nails, splashed some perfume on myself, and put on a clean, white silk nightdress. Juhani was watching TV. I went into the bedroom, whispered goodbye to the children, and got into bed. Juhani came in much later, complained that he didn't dare touch me anymore since I'd gotten so strange. I said that a beautiful corpse is more pleasing to the Lord and one's family than an ugly one. I could see that Juhani thought it was all a lot of nonsense. He looked anxious and didn't want to talk anymore, didn't even want to look at me. I fell asleep, then, and stepped out into a courtyard full of white flowers, and my mood was light and easy.

FOREIGN

THE SUN WAS SHINING BEHIND THE FACTORY, COLORING THE
water turquoise by the shore. A boy stood barefoot on the pier
with a broom in his hands, squinting in the sunlight. On the
pier there were chunks of meat being washed by small waves.
The planks were sticky with blood, and white blubber floated
on the edge of the shore in long strips. The boy felt small and
dejected. The boat was already three days late when it came in
wearily from the sea with its white sides soiled by death. All
morning the boy had stood watching as great, foul-smelling
heaps of fish were lifted from the hold. The dockworkers had
taken off their shirts and got stained with blood as they carried
the hunks of meat from the pier to the factory's freezing plant.
The boy dipped the broom in the water and swept some of the
congealed blood off the large fish. He felt sad. All these ice-cov-
ered mountains, surrounded by water on every side, the sticky
blood and stinking meat would be his fate, too. He would live
only in order to lose his life. He gathered the chunks in a plastic box, carried it into the factory, and washed the blood from
his feet with cold water.

THE BAR IS RECTANGULAR. LONG AND NARROW. SMALL LAMPS hang on the walls, surrounded by heavy, gray smoke. At the counter there are drunken fishermen, sailors talking in foreign languages, and large-breasted, second-class whores. Everyone talks a lot, as low and indistinctly as possible. The place is almost dark, with teenage car thieves, drug-pushers, and senile pensioners who can hardly walk anymore. Two monks in black habits appear at the door. Straight-backed and dignified. One of them wipes the slush from his shoulders, the other touches a crucifix that hangs around his neck, as if to make sure that his faith is still intact. The monks step up to the counter with the skill born of experience and order double whiskeys from the tired blonde bargirl, then take their glasses to the front of the bar, behind the rabid Eskimo fishermen. One of them digs a pipe out of the inner pocket of his habit, fills and lights it, gulps down half of his glass, and glances at a beer bottle that comes flying across the room and crashes against the wall opposite.

The other opens his mouth to say something, but closes it again and smiles to himself. The monks go over to get second, third, and fourth double whiskeys. The one with the pipe has another pipeful, and they go on their way. In the street, right in front of the bar, a man lies bloodstained and half-covered by slush. The leather-gloved bouncer looks at the monks and says that's what happens to guys who kick other guys in the balls. The monks start to walk up the street and reach the top of the small hill. There they can see over the whole town, and even the waves of the Atlantic, like in old photographs. They check into a five-star hotel, and order breakfast and the morning papers for the next day. They take the elevator to a double room on the fourth floor and make themselves at home. They slowly take off their heavy habits and hang them carefully on white hangers. One of them opens a bottle of Jim Beam. The monks sit in their underwear and have two more slugs of whiskey each. Together they wash, and then sink tired but happy into the white silk sheets of the soft waterbed.

THE CHURCH STOOD IN RUINS. THE STEEPLE HAD COLLAPSED years ago, the windows were covered by plywood boards, and the rotted plank doors creaked in the wind. The stone glaciers that surrounded the church gleamed brightly in the winter sun, and the clouds floated in white masses along the mountain slopes. The woman who was approaching the church prayed to the sun for a moment of peace—her eyes hurt. The day had been long and unpredictable. In the morning she had felt a strange unease, had quickly eaten her cold breakfast, and set off without knowing where to. Now she entered the church. There was snow on the floor, on the altar and the rickety pews. When she stopped in front of the altarpiece, she suddenly remembered the dream. The wind tugged at the rotted doors, and the snow began to whirl in. The wind pulled at the altar, blowing loose anything around it. It blew the woman over onto the floor in front of the altar. Through a crack in the plywood boards she watched as black horses came plunging out of the snowy darkness, surrounded the church, and tried to force their way in through the doors. She managed to close them, and the horses reared up in panic against one another, striking their hooves against the walls, which were worn by ice and rain. They neighed in terrible fear, their eyes large and watery. The woman prayed to the sun to come back and kill the storm, and at the same moment the Christ on the cross began to bleed. The blood bubbled red and thick under the dust and the thin layers of ice. It flowed slowly along the wall and down onto the altarpiece, melting red holes in the snow. The black horses vanished, the snowstorm became a sunny afternoon and the church was as it had been before. The snow was pure and white and there was no blood to be seen on the altarpiece.

When he'd thrown earth on the coffin in the name of the Father, the Son, and the Holy Ghost, he went into the sacristy, changed out of his canonical garb into a black monk's habit, and put a skullcap on his head. He stood in front of me for a moment, smiling, took a large gulp of the red wine in the communion cup, and belched. We went out through the back door, leaving the church's pompous façade behind us. We walked through the town. We waded through snowdrifts and slipped in icy courtyards. He walked slightly ahead of me, his black habit scraping the ground. The house was yellow and old; the concrete steps had almost disappeared under a thick layer of snow. In the doorway he made a little sign of the cross, and then we stepped inside. On the outside of the door hung a wind-lashed icon. I didn't take my coat off—it was cold in there. I sat down at the kitchen table and looked out across a backyard full of junk. He put some water on to boil, went to the liquor cabinet and served up hot rum and honey. The bedroom was behind the kitchen; a short and narrow wooden bed, a leather-bound Bible on the bedside table, two white candles in pewter candle-holders, floral patterned wallpaper on the walls, and a small window, from which one could see red, snow-covered cars. I got into the bed and pressed myself under a thick, cold, damp heap of blankets. He sat down beside me, stroked my hair for a moment, and then crawled under the blankets without taking off his habit. There wasn't much room in the bed, and the mattress felt hard. He kissed my eyes, touched my throat and sought my lips. I kicked my woolen socks off, and he did likewise. I threw my woolen sweater to the floor, and he threw off his skull-cap. He pulled off my layers of clothing, and I lay naked in the damp sheets. He didn't smile, but his eyes showed what he was thinking. I lit the candles—in the midday sun their light was almost invisible. He quickly took off his trousers but kept on his habit and the thick metal cross around his neck. He had long, coal-black hair, a curly, clean, well-cut beard, and chalk-white hands. He entered me. It was more violent than receiving a stab in the chest with a knife. The blood flowed, I kissed him and took his handsome penis in my hand, and it grew into a Tower of Babel between my thighs. We lay in the hard, narrow bed until the next morning. Then he had to go to the sacristy again through the back door and change out of the monk's habit into his canonical clothes in order to throw earth on the dead.

BETWEEN THE CENTER OF TOWN AND THE BOARDING HOUSE THERE was a large marsh. The February frosts that came in from the Atlantic had frozen it into a glistening field. The woman was walking straight towards the boarding house. She was dressed in a fur coat and high leather boots, and her face bore an irritated expression. In the sky, the trail of a jet plane ran against dark blue clouds. As she passed some bushes, the woman slowed. She felt a pain and remembered something very far away. It was the middle of summer: a thick green lawn and a pig screaming in the slaughterer's hands. The woman could place the memory. It had happened in another place, in another country, but it had happened. Her expression grew sad. She stuck her hands deep in her coat pockets and felt the cold begin to rise from her belly up towards her hair.

The man behind the bushes held his breath and waited for the moment, when the woman would be in exactly the right place. His eyes had a fearful look, and the veins at his temples were swollen. He waited quietly, a little longer, and then attacked the woman from behind. The woman fell on her back, hitting her head on the ice. The man was panting. A pale, childish face, fair, streaming hair and black leather gloves. The man hit the woman in the face and tore the fur coat open, forced his hand inside her blouse and tried to pull her jeans open. The woman didn't scream, but looked at the man attentively. The man actually seemed handsome to her. She looked up at the sky. The white trail of the jet plane was gone. There were only the blue clouds and the cold, which made her nipples stand upright.

"Let's do it somewhere where it's warm," the woman said as the man tugged desperately at her tight jeans. The man started and pulled his hand away. He stared at the woman suspiciously, but let go of her hands, from which a little blood was trickling.

"I only have a small room, but it's warm."

The man looked at the woman's swollen lips and then got off of her. She staggered to her feet, buttoned up her blouse, and straightened her hair. Then she continued on her way towards the boarding house. The man followed, several steps behind her.

The concierge was asleep. They went to an unpretentious

room on the ground floor and took off their clothes, the woman expertly, the man clumsily. The woman threw off the blankets, lay down, and looked the man in the eyes. There was nothing in them except a deep emptiness. The woman sighed, put his hand between her thighs, closed her eyes, and tried a little smile. The man lowered himself shyly onto her. The woman caressed his shoulders. The man kissed the woman's breasts and neck, tried to penetrate her, but without success. The woman closed her eyes and swallowed. The man turned over beside her and whimpered like a puppy. They slept in each other's arms until morning; then the woman had to go to work. She took a package of cigarettes from her night table. After midday the man woke up with a start and left the room without looking back.

THE MAN WITH THE MITER ON HIS HEAD STARTED A SILVER-GRAY
1959 Maserati in front of a port terminal in the west harbor
and turned its nose east. There was a woman sitting beside the
monk. Blue-black hair, an Eskimo face, slender legs. They
drove along the narrow, icy road by the fjord, stopped at a
gas station, drank tepid coffee, and smoked cigarettes. They
passed trucks that smelled of rotten fish. They passed Ladas
that drew long clouds of exhaust behind them and giant-
wheeled GMC pickups that turned the furrows in the road to
slush.

The house was far away from everything, close to a deep
ravine. They left the car in a warm garage that had been built by
the side of the road and walked up to the house. The monk had
four plastic bags, the woman a leather suitcase with wheels.
The courtyard was deserted, but lights burned in the house's
eight rooms. The woman took off her leopard-skin coat, left it
on the sofa, and sat down in front of the TV. The monk spread

out the contents of the plastic bags on the kitchen sideboard, put a cassette in the Bang & Olufsen VCR, and pressed a button on the remote. The picture was sharp and the colors were right. The woman lit a long Winston cigarette and immersed herself in the film's tropical landscapes.

The monk put his miter on the coffee table, his black habit in the wardrobe, slipped on his red Zig-Zag sweatpants and a football shirt with Public Enemy on the back, quietly walked to the kitchen, switched on the Philips De Luxe microwave oven, and spent a long time fiddling with the Moulinexes, Krupses, Mieles, and Zanussis. Cool Key was rapping from the radio on top of the Rosenlew refrigerator. The rhythm blended pleasantly with the wild jungle noises from the video. Just after eleven, dinner was ready. The monk set the table with black plates and fetched two bottles of Aloxe Cortone 1978 from the cellar.

The woman approached the table lazily. The monk pulled out a chair for her. The video was still playing, but the monk switched off Cool Key.

"Such a naively theistic image of God fails to answer the existential questions of postmodern man," said the woman, as she bit into her steak.

"That's why I've sought a solution through contemplation," said the monk, trying to catch the woman's eye. The woman stared at her bloody steak.

"If it gives you solace."

After the meal the monk put the dishes in his Zanussi dishwasher, washed and polished the Krups blender, the Moulinex kitchen assistant, the Miele mixer, and the espresso machine, and tidied the kitchen. When he was done, he took an unopened bottle of 1956 Puttony Tokay under his arm and went into the living room, where the woman lay on the sofa, asleep under her fur coat. He turned off the whirring video, threw himself into an armchair, and sat there until five in the morning with a look of depressed contemplation.

LATE ONE NIGHT I WENT DOWNTOWN TO LOOK FOR NICK CAVE,
but what I ended up with was something quite different. A fat
red-faced fisherman from the east coast. I undressed him,
talked beautifully to him about love, the stars, and the earth's
gravity. He listened with his big ears pricked up, smiling an innocent, idiotic smile. He wanted everything, and right away. I
did my best to oblige. Next morning he was gurgling like a
newly fed infant in the creaking double bed of the hotel room,
wanting more. I smiled and whispered sweetly in his ear. I let
him enter me, but at the same moment I grabbed him by the
throat and squeezed as hard as I could. There was a wheezing,
and the life slipped out of his fat body. I got up, dressed, ordered
breakfast, and left.

THE GOOD FRIDAY CHURCH BELLS THUNDERED IN THE LANES
of the small fishing village. The man from Morocco opened a
gilt-wrapped Easter egg in the communal kitchen of the fish
factory hostel. The hostel was quiet and empty. The man bit a
piece of the chocolate egg, put it down on the table, and looked
at his wristwatch. He quickly crumpled the gilt wrapping,
threw it into the wastepaper basket and went into his room on
the other side of the hall. Everything seemed to be ready. On the
armchair a gray, tattered robe, on the bed an executioner's
hood, and on the floor two foot-rags from the days of the
wartime depression. The man put on the robe, pulled the hood
over his head, and checked in the mirror to see that it was prop-
erly fastened. He bound the foot-rags carefully around his black
leather shoes and then left the room. Outside the front door lay
a large plastic cross on which a tree pattern had been clumsily
painted. The man threw the cross on his shoulder and walked
with swift steps towards the small fishing village, from where

the procession was to start. The harbor was deserted. The man looked around him, smoked a cigarette, and spat on the quay before setting off. Seagulls flew very low in large, white flocks, almost silent. The cross bounced up and down on his shoulder; the weather was sunny and calm. He walked quickly along the street, his back bent and his gaze turned to the ground. People rushed out of their houses like lightning and everywhere there was anguished shouting and groaning. The seagulls screamed, the women began to shriek like pigs being slaughtered, and the men waved their arms as if to grab at their last hope. The children's faces were contorted. The man staggered onwards, hobbling along in his tattered robe, and finally collapsed under the weight of his cross. A man in a blue suit and white shirt ran forward in tears from the crowd to help the cross-bearer. He took the cross on his shoulders, but looked as though he was about to collapse under the burden himself. The crowd followed the two men and cries of anguish echoed along the icy slopes of the mountain. The church was six hundred meters away. The people stood thronging the steps up to it, for only the man in the hood was allowed to go inside. When the man in the blue suit, with a compassionate look on his face, had closed the church doors behind the man with the cross, the people stopped wailing. They dried their tears and hurried home laughing and joking to eat the roast mutton that should now be ready. Exhausted, the man threw down the cross in the church's vestry, went to the pulpit and quickly undressed. After that he went into the toilet, slicked his hair with gel and then walked back to the hostel in jeans and a black leather jacket. He sat down at the kitchen table and ate the other half of the chocolate egg.

FIVE MEN SAT AROUND THE TABLE. THE OLDEST TOOK OUT A pack of whalebone cards and dealt them. No one spoke; the men played very quickly, without looking at one another. Their faces were serious and the tobacco smoke in the room was thick. With each round, the pile of money grew larger. The old man lost as usual. Not because he wasn't good, but because he no longer knew his own place. Once he'd been king, but now he was a beggar. He looked at his fellow players; they were young men who had their whole lives ahead of them. They radiated strength, health, and greed. The old man knew that by the end of the last round he would have lost everything, and would have become a different person. His money floated away into the others' pockets. The young men didn't smile, even though they had reason to, but maintained a serious expression of moderate respect. The lights were switched off, and they went outside. The night felt damp and heavy. They walked along the slushy street towards the center of town, each thinking to himself about his own wins and losses. The old man fell behind the others. That was easy, because he was the biggest loser. Watching the young men's broad shoulders and powerful arms, he felt even more inadequate than before. He touched the pistol that hung at his hip, lit a cigarette, smoked it, and carefully drew the weapon. No one noticed anything. He shot all four of them from behind, along the street. The blood flowed, staining the slush red. The old man went over to the fallen corpses; the holes in their chests looked very small and modest. He checked to see that they were all dead, and then put the pistol in his mouth.

WHILE THE SOLDIERS AT THE MILITARY BASE WERE PUTTING on their leather suits and flying boots, the man entered his house, took off his scarf, put it on the kitchen table, and kissed the woman who never smiled. The woman sat on a stool next to the freezer, looking at him. He gave her a handful of bright yellow pills and she swallowed them quickly and mechanically. She was unusually pretty, young and neurotic. The man took a sandwich box out of the refrigerator and an electric lamp from the closet and stuffed them into a small backpack. Then he fastened a thin leather collar round the woman's neck, attached a long gold chain to the collar, and fixed the other end of the chain to the handle of the freezer door. The woman watched all his movements closely. The man took three small medicine bottles from his pocket and arranged the pills in three rows on the window ledge, glanced at the woman, raised his index finger, said "Now, then," took the backpack and left, because he had to get to the edge of the glacier before it got dark. When the sound of his footsteps was gone, the woman sat down on the floor. She held the chain in her hand, squinted up at a narrow strip of sky, and wondered who the black-clad man was who kept entering her apartment and her life, this strange man in white frills whose visits were so rare. Perhaps he was an alien from another galaxy, a well-meaning angel who looked like a devil. This idea calmed her, and as she let her heavy eyelids close, she felt very happy. Fifteen gray-green surveillance helicopters appeared in the sky. They formed a silent plough that quickly moved east, throwing a black, bird-like shadow over the city.

I RAN INTO HIM ONE MORNING AT ABOUT SIX AT A BUS STOP outside town. He was black, and he was carrying five large plastic bags of stuff, and a bongo drum on his back. He asked if I was going to the east coast. Watery sleet was falling. We sat on our bags and smoked imported American cigarettes. The bus was two hours late. He was from the savannahs of Central Africa, somewhere close to the Zaire border. He'd arrived seven days ago on a boat and planned to stay. Why, he couldn't explain. We sat in the bus half-asleep for eleven hours. Through snowstorm, rain, and sun. Late in the evening we arrived at a small port town. The main street was deserted, the store windows dark. The only light came from an oil company's enormous glowing sign on the side of the mountain. We got a double room together behind the fish factory. A large window, a stained, flea-infested coconut mat and two iron bedsteads. In the morning we went to the fish factory, but didn't get hired. Him because he was too black and his build too primitive; me because I was with him. For three days we stayed in our beds under thick layers of blankets, drinking instant coffee and rolling cigarettes. He got depressed by the landscape of frozen stones and yearned for the African sun. I preferred to forget about the past and not plan for the future. On the fourth morning we took the bus back to the capital. A neon-blue sun was shining over the Atlantic, and I knew that life was going to be different.

THE MAN FOCUSED THE CAMERA AND TOOK A PICTURE. A MOMENT later the camera spat out a black, rectangular piece of paper that he handed to the woman, smiling.

"If you wait a minute, the photo will develop."

The woman tossed back her long, curly hair and stared skeptically at the piece of paper.

"It'll be developed soon."

The woman looked at the man suspiciously and lowered her eyes to the black piece of paper.

"Did I look nice?"

"You do," the man replied, running his tongue across his dry lips.

A moment's silence. Coming out from under the woman's small bikini were a pair of coffee-brown breasts, a small belly, and buttocks that were almost imperceptible to the eye. The man desired the woman, as everyone lying on the beach could see. The woman shifted her feet. She started to look bored.

"Nothing's going to happen. It's black, and it's going to stay black."

"You're right," he replied, snatching the black paper from her and tossing it to the ground. The woman took his hand and they ran off along the shoreline all the way to the rocks, where they burst into breathless laughter and began to kiss each other.

When the beach was empty, a young girl in a white cardigan strolled along the shore and found the photo. It showed a blue sea and a pretty woman with small breasts in a black bikini. The woman was smiling. The girl looked at the photo for a long time, felt a strange pleasure, and without so much as looking round, she put it in the pocket of her dress and went home. There she sat quietly, and as her father switched off the TV and her mother flushed the toilet, she undressed, took the picture of the woman out from under the mattress, and kissed it.

THIS IS MY LAND, THAT FJORD, THOSE MOUNTAINS, AND ALL the ravines between them. When I was a child the wind came in from the Atlantic, raw and whistling. I used to jump into the ravine and go down to the stream, where it was sheltered and quiet, like at the bottom of a bottle. This landscape has never given me any rest. My father had no mercy. He forced me to go to sea on long, cold fishing trips, and to eat raw, freshly caught fish. My father was strong in faith and will and even in his grave has never left me in peace but keeps trying to return to the land of the living. Short, tough, and cruel. That's how I remember him in the rough-grained landscape of my childhood.

My mother never existed. Only occasionally did I catch a glimpse of her when she left the kitchen and came down to the yard. She would walk along the little path to the fjord to fetch dried fish, then disappear. I don't know who my mother was, I don't know where she came from or where she went. I grew up to be a man without will or strength. I am pursued by the dead. I am running for my life. The ravines of my childhood have filled with sand, the mountains have crumbled into the fjord, and the fjord has drained into the sea.

ON CHRISTMAS DAY REFRACTED LIGHTS BURNED YELLOW IN
every house, and even in the courtyards Christmas bulbs had
been hung, blinking on and off and gently twinkling. The man
went out—the atmosphere in the small, low-ceilinged room
oppressed him. The streets were deserted and covered with
fresh snow. The man walked down to the harbor. In the midst
of all the melted slush it looked gray and sad. The oil tanks, the
loading bays, the motionless cranes; white swans pecking at
swollen, shapeless pieces of bread in the foul-smelling shore
water. The man passed the loading port, which was full of con-
tainers and long-haul trucks, and walked up the hill towards
the foot of the mountain slope. He planned to climb to the top
—perhaps there he would see himself more clearly. The slope
was icy. The man had to crawl upward on all fours, swaying
from time to time and even falling a few meters. Soon darkness
fell. The lights of the town shrank to small, dim points down in
the valley, and the man felt a great fear descend on him. Then

came the first gusts of wind, and in a moment the mountain slope was enveloped in blinding, whirling snow. It lashed his face with needles of ice. He tried to shield his face but the wind pulled at him with increasing force. He fell sobbing to the ground and felt despair and hopelessness. The mountaintop had disappeared, like the harbor and the town. There was nothing but icy needles, pitch-black infinity and death wanting to consume him.

The man woke up with a start. He was surrounded by white light and had curled up into a little bundle under a thick layer of snow. He got up and saw the yellow moon lighting up the mountaintop and the stars that showed the way back to the town. His blood flowed burning in his veins, but his heart was light. He shook the snow out of his hair and shoes and walked calmly back down to the deserted, Christmas-twinkling town.

SHE ARRIVED IN TOWN A WEEK AGO, BUT I HAVEN'T SEEN HER once. I don't know why I don't want to see her. I avoid the center of town, don't go around the streets or the pubs in the evening, since I don't want to bump into her out of the blue. I don't like the fact that she's forced herself on my country and my town. This is the only world I have and I don't want her ruining it. She came and rang the doorbell. I didn't put out the lights, but I didn't open the door either. She knew I was home. A piece of paper fell in through the letterbox, with the name of the hotel and a phone number. I looked at the paper for a long time, and then threw it in the wastebasket. It's been three years since I left her. I wanted to be the cowboy who goes away without saying goodbye, promising that he'll return some day. But I had no plans to return then, and I have none now. I left her because I wanted to live alone. I don't like other people's smells, their surprising facial expressions or awkward way of sitting at the dinner table or in front of the TV. I want to live alone, because I don't need anyone, least of all a woman who makes everything little thing into a problem. And here I am, sitting in this armchair, in a cramped basement room for the seventh day in a row, thinking about her all the time. I can't get a moment's rest, because she's always here. It makes me so excited that I can't sleep. My heart beats in the back of my head and the tips of my fingers. It excites me to know that she's in town, at a hotel close by, and I'm down here in a stuffy basement. Of course I could very easily release my excitement by unzipping my trousers and taking it out, but I won't do that. I want to prolong this torment for as long as she's in town. I want to enjoy every second she spends in town. I'll torment myself by keeping the excitement alive and only when she's flown back to her own country will I show myself any mercy.

EVER SINCE THE LUMBERJACKING WORK RAN OUT, I'VE DONE the same thing every Wednesday afternoon. I get the empty beer bottles together in the sink and then load them into a plastic bag. I take the bag across the yard, out onto the icy main road and down to where the grocery van pulls in. Today the weather looks unusually promising, there's hardly any frost, and the sun is shining obliquely from the southwest out over the snowy fields. A man and two women are already waiting. The man also has a bag of empty bottles. We stand in silence, side by side, as we usually do. No one has anything new to report. What could happen in a week? A week, a month, a year? Old and slow, the grocery van turns the corner of the road and stops in front of us. The grocer drives with the same old indifferent expression; there are gaps between his teeth and the ones that are left are in bad shape, just like mine. He has a sunken chest and there are deep wrinkles around his eyes. I take sixteen bottles of Lapinkulta out of the crate, the way I always do, and put my ration card up on top of the engine, which serves as a counter. I dig the money out of my pocket and drop it in the grocer's hand. My finances have dwindled—I've gone from paper to coin. The grocer counts the money, and I'm content; life always feels more positive with sixteen unopened beers in my bag. The grocer looks at me: "You're fifteen pennies short—what, you can't count that high?" I leave, go back down along the road, saying I'm heading home to get the missing money. He doesn't even nod, just keeps the same expression. I realize that it's a matter of life or death. I get the missing coins out of the coffee tin, take the hunting rifle out from under the bed, and go back to the van. The women are still standing there, turning rye loaves in their hands. I give the grocer the fifteen pennies and he glares at me with malicious satisfaction. I lift the rifle and see his expression change—surprised but self-assured. I fire before any of the customers can blink. The women stuff their shopping bags without so much as a look at the grocer's bloody corpse, and then leave. I grab the bagful of beers, shoulder my rifle, and walk home. It's time for afternoon coffee, but since this day has turned out a bit different, I decide to have a beer instead. I sit down at the kitchen table, and enjoy the hiss when the cap comes off the bottle, and the full, strong taste of malt.

THIS HAPPENED ON THURSDAY EVENING LAST WEEK, EXACTLY as expected: I came home from work and tied myself up in the leather armchair, like I've done every Thursday evening for the past five years, if I haven't been on a business trip or if something else hasn't gotten in the way. I drove home from work, read the newspaper at the kitchen table, drank a glass of whiskey, drew the Venetian blinds, and switched on the small table lamp with the dim bulb. I undressed, hung my suit on a clothes hanger and sat down in the armchair. I breathed deeply and calmly, relaxed all over and swept away all the worldly dross that had gathered up in me during the week. I took a rope from the closet and also turned on the light in the fish tank that stands directly opposite my armchair. I tied myself up in the chair, as tightly and painfully as possible. The rings of fat on my belly bulged out between the coils of rope, which also pressed so hard on my chest that my breath only came in jerks. I drew the end of the rope round my penis and testicles, and in under my buttocks, and made it so tight that drops of sweat rose on my forehead. I sat for a long time without moving, forcing myself to think of the most bizarre and painful methods of torture I could imagine, and felt great satisfaction. I imagined the commandant of a concentration camp pushing his rifle into a Jewish girl, I imagined a mercenary in the jungle cutting the throat of an old man who was babbling and pleading for mercy. It felt so calming after a hard day of work at the office. With my free hand I got a little fruit knife out from under the cushion and began making small cuts on the inside of my thighs and lower abdomen. It felt purifying. The old wounds hadn't healed yet. There were lots of them along my thighs, but the rest of my body was untouched, the wounds were only on the insides of my thighs and on my lower stomach. The blood flowed in neat little trickles along my legs and warmed them nicely. I put the knife away in the armchair again, fell asleep, and had a dream:

It was a hot day in June. I came home from work and felt happy. My wife greeted me. I wanted to kiss her but she pushed me away. She screamed obscenities at me, ranted and raved, showered me with abuse, and at last attacked me with her bare hands. I took hold of her arm, dragged her into the bedroom, put a gag in her mouth, and tied her to the wardrobe. Then I fetched a bow and arrow from the attic. Her eyes grew wide with terror and pain. The sweat dripped from her temples, but in the end she had no idea what was coming. I closed the Venetian blinds, positioned myself a couple of meters away from her and drew the bow. One last terrified gaze, and the arrow cleaved the air. It passed straight through her skull and stuck in the wardrobe door.

I woke up. The blood had dried in red stripes on my legs, and my buttocks had stuck to the black leather. I lifted them, and the end of the rope came loose. Then I freed myself from the straitjacket, hid the rope in the wardrobe, and went into the shower. I sang a folk song and washed myself with oil of balsam. I felt calm and good. After the shower I disinfected the wounds and treated them with natural herb lotion. I put on a blue suit, opened the Venetian blinds, and poured myself another whiskey.

TONIGHT I AM GOING TO FIND MYSELF A MAN. NOT BECAUSE I need one, but because today is the first time I'm wearing the black lace-patterned body stocking I bought in Paris, which accentuates my breasts and the pretty curve of my hips. I want a man because this evening I need an audience to witness me in the most elegant European underclothes money can buy. So I go into the hotel bar, order a Campari, and choose a man with a cool gaze, gray temples, and a quiet air. I take him to his hotel room, order a large bottle of champagne and some Russian caviar. I offer him a light and he hurries to unfasten my garters. Then I let him take off my red dress and I stretch and smile generously on the sofa. He hangs his jacket on a clothes hanger, puts his white shirt on the arm of the chair, folds his striped trousers with care, and puts them in the wardrobe. He lies down beside me and says: "You smell wonderful." I smile and have another glass of champagne. There's still the petticoat, but he doesn't know how to take that off. I get up and stand in the middle of the room, and the wall-to-wall carpeting seems to sway under my feet. Slowly and voluptuously, I let the black petticoat fall, and there I stand in the world's most elegant underwear, like a beautiful statue. He looks at me admiringly and greedily. He looks for a long time and I stand there, caressed by the warm stream of air in the room for what feels like an eternity. Then he comes towards me like a conqueror and holds me in a firm embrace. I tear myself free of his hot arms, snatch up my dress, my petticoat, and shoes, and run out into the hall. I go into the bathroom on the ground floor—luckily I don't meet anyone— put my clothes back on, and feel extraordinarily happy. I put on more powder and lipstick, and walk up to the doorman in a relaxed, matter-of-fact way. With a deep bow he hands me my fur coat and with a yawn I go out to the first taxi that comes along.

THE MAN SITS IN A SYNTHETIC LEATHER ARMCHAIR IN A LIVING room lit by a bright neon strip. The dusty porcelain objects on the hardwood bookshelves against the far wall compete in vain with the sharp contrast of the TV screen. It's an hour after midnight and he pretends to be staring at the screen. A red light is coming in at the window, passing through the doorway and hitting the trashy painting on the wall. The man tries to change his position but it doesn't ease the tension in his muscles. He picks up the remote from the floor and fast-forwards to the image of a black-skinned woman sticking a cucumber into herself. He moves his hand to his limp penis and fingers it gently. The expression of the woman in the picture is one of bliss, and her mouth says oooh. The man feels his limp penis go rigid inside his acrylic sweatpants and in a moment it grows to full size. He swallows and looks at the bedroom door. It is white and closed. The man turns back to the screen and stares at the woman's enormous breasts. He puts his hands inside his pants and takes hold of his rigid penis, beats it against his flabby stomach as he keeps an eye on the bedroom door. The black woman swallows the last inch of the cucumber and moans, the man strains hurriedly with an anxious look on his face, and the synthetic leather armchair creaks. The black woman is replaced by a white man who is traveling somewhere in the dense jungles of Africa. The man puts his limp, wet penis back in his trousers, holds his breath for a moment, and turns off the TV. He sits there for a while, feeling himself relax all the way from his head to his toes. The red light has moved past the painting now and is moving towards the armchair. He yawns, tenderly strokes his belly and his flabby chest, gets up and goes to the bedroom door, opens it cautiously, and disappears into the summer coolness of the dark room.

I TOOK AN OFF-SEASON FLIGHT TO HELSINKI AND BOUGHT A MAN right at the airport. He had brown eyes and broad shoulders, with perhaps a bit too much weight around the middle. His face was average and he had a kind of boyish look. He wasn't really what I wanted, but at least he was a man. We checked into a hotel and I made sure I got my money's worth. I lay on my back, I crouched on all fours, I bent over the table, I sat on the sofa, I stood leaning against the wall. Then I paid him, and gave him twenty extra as a bonus for a job well done, then sent him away. After that I took a nice bath, and ordered some women's magazines and sparkling wine. I read the magazines and gradually polished off the whole bottle. Then I got dressed and went to my seminar in Otaniemi. I stayed there for two hours, put my name on the list, and smiled at the head of department. Then I went to the theater, then on to a nightclub for a drink, and finally headed back to the soft double bed at the hotel.

Next morning I flew home and told my husband it had been a routine business trip. He believed me.

I PICKED HER UP IN THE BAR OF THE FENNIA RESTAURANT. She wore a Valintalo T-shirt that showed everything, and a threadbare skirt. She took me back to her place and treated me as though I'd won a gold medal in a dog show, and I enjoyed it, an old urban cowboy like myself really deserved it. All my life, I've always driven myself to the limits, further than all the other people here in Southwest Finland put together. I've slept in hostelries that no one else would ever set foot in, for decades I've sat in smoky bars tormented by the fumes of greasy cooking, drinking beer by the crate. I've slept with my boots on in Sinebrychoff Park in the summer and munched hot dogs in abandoned railway stations. I've raped little girls in Kajsaniemi Park in the middle of the coldest winters, so you could say that I more than deserved a woman's tender care after all that. Sixteen weeks is just right. In that time even a guy in a completely hopeless condition can rehabilitate himself and get back on track. Then I set off with my pockets full of money and my backpack full of food. And the woman and her three kids waved cheerfully from a balcony on the fifth floor.

"I GREW TIRED OF HUMAN BEINGS AND THE WORLD. I'D HAD ENOUGH of noise, shouting stockbrokers, innocent young bank clerks, and insurance executives always making all kinds of demands."

The two men sit in silence on a small black leather sofa in the middle of a light, high-ceilinged room. On the other side of the street, the clean lines of Manhattan's skyscrapers grow towards a sky overcast with a thick layer of cloud.

"I lived one life there, and began another life here. There was too much of everything there, while here there's not enough of anything, and that's good. When I came here I took this hotel room and decided to care for only myself. I didn't send my address to anyone. I have managed to live in total isolation from the outside world and I am happier than ever. Human beings and the world outside remain distant, and comfortably alien."

The man in the blue suit gets up from the sofa and goes over to the window. For a long time he looks down at the swarming street below, lit by streetlamps and advertising signs, where black men search for newspapers to use as blankets and white men in doorways stick needles into their veins.

103

"I tried to meet all the demands that were made of me. I was always on the job, as a husband, as a lover, as a father, and even when I was asleep at night. You can't go on doing that indefinitely. So I came here."

The men clink their glasses for friendship's sake and smile stiffly. The only sound that can be heard in the air-conditioned hotel room is a flat humming. The man in the blue suit undoes the top button of his shirt and loosens the knot of his tie. He longs to be home, back with his wife at the breakfast table.

"Here I allow myself everything. I serve myself just as once upon a time I served people who were ready to take everything and not give me a thing in return."

The man in the blue suit feels anxious while at the same time completely empty. For a while he thinks about the life he'd once wanted to live, looks surreptitiously at the other man and clears his throat stiffly.

"Once I too was . . ." he begins, but the words freeze on his lips.

The other man looks up from the white wall-to-wall carpet, presses a button on his remote and finds a football game on TV.

THE GIRL SAT POUTING IN THE KITCHEN AND BEFORE I EVEN GOT
as far as the hallway she called me over. I saw right away that she
was the party's "hot blonde," the one I'm always looking for.
She said she was from some small town, had a pink complexion
and a body like a fashion model. She wanted to eat well and ex-
pensively, so we went out, and I paid. She wanted to go to my
apartment to admire the ocean view, and so I called a taxi. In the
back seat she swayed against my shoulder, giggling the way
small-town girls do. She drank my whiskey; she smoked the
last of my cigarettes, and switched off the record player just as
my favorite song was coming on. She carelessly ran her hands
over the household gadgets in the kitchen and ate a whole tin of
caviar with her fingers. She sprawled on the leather sofa in her
red miniskirt and tried to look as bored as possible. By the time
she opened her mouth and told me to carry her to the waterbed
and fuck her, I was totally turned off. I said that enough was
enough, that I'd been paying for her all night, and that I wasn't

105

just a piece of meat. I made her adopt lotus position on the Afghan rug and gave her a nine-hour lecture on Taoism. It went right over her pretty little model's head, but I wouldn't let her go. I had a right to get something for the money I'd spent on her. I let her out the next day at about one. She looked really hot as she rushed to the bus stop as though escaping from a sex murderer, screaming that I was the worst pervert she'd ever met.

I GOT OUT OF THE HANDCUFFS ON FRIDAY MORNING. THEY GAVE me a rail ticket to Helsinki and I was at the station well before noon. I caught a streetcar to the dealership on Mannerheim Street and took the latest model Mercedes out for a test drive. I drove to Paula's place in Vuosaari and let myself in with my key. I took a carton of milk from the fridge and drank it as if my life depended on it. I called Paula at work and she guessed it was me right away. She got a taxi and came over. We had coffee, Paula made toasted sandwiches, and then we fucked in the armchair. She giggled the way she always does when she sees me. It had been a while, at least three months, and it showed. I was horny and so was she. Then she stuffed some underwear and a black evening dress into a bag, we got in the car, she set herself in the front seat like a peacock, and I stepped on the gas. She thought I'd made a good choice—she likes big white cars. I drove to the Katajanokka Casino and checked that there was no one on guard, then smashed the kitchen window and ran to the bar. I took twenty bottles of whiskey, and ten more out of the storage room. Bacardi rum, cognac, a crate of light beer, four crates of strong beer, and a case of Finncream for Paula. I stuck them in the trunk and we drove to Lohja. The weather was great, just a slight frost, and we dropped in at the best hotel en route for chateaubriand steaks and mashed potatoes. A bottle of wine from my inside pocket, and we had it made. I was free. I had the world's sweetest woman, a car, and a carload of booze. Paula paid the bill. I drove to Turku, we booked a suite at Socis, I brought in some of the booze and opened it. We had a really great time. I drank Napoleon and Paula had Bacardi and Pepsi. Then we fucked for a bit, front and back, had something to eat, and then fucked some more. Paula's body was fantastic, and what tits! They were like melons. Next morning we drove to Jyväskylä, drinking all the way. I went so fast we were just a blur on the highway. We were going well over two hundred and Paula tittered in her seat. At Jyväskylä we checked into the Cumulus, but we didn't like it there and only stayed two hours. I gave her a quick poke, and then we ate and took off to Oulu. We were dead tired when we got there. I parked right outside the main door of Hotel Vaakuna and we hurried up to the ninth floor. We ordered the best that room service had to offer and fell asleep before they'd brought us anything. On Sunday we headed back to Helsinki. Paula's Visa card showed several hundred minus signs, and I realized that I'd have to sell the car, my white dream. I took it to Lehtisaari. It went for a song, but at least I got some cash. What a fucking crook the buyer was, he didn't ask for proof of ownership or anything. Bought it because he was getting it for practically nothing—though I have to admit that he'd softened me up quite a bit earlier that evening, in the Golden Ox bar, where we discussed the deal. He really did get it cheap, but I'm not just a sucker. I'll help a friend in need, and of course a businessman needs more than just a white dream. Paula and I flew to Joensuu, and I screwed her. What tits, I'm telling you. Then it was Monday morning and she flew to her job in Helsinki. I stayed on in Joensuu for another day, resting. In the evening I flew to Helsinki and the cops were at the airport to meet me. It was no big deal, I was a little surprised, maybe, but after all they had plenty of reasons to throw me in the Black Maria and take me off to Paasila. I slept there for days. Man, I was far-gone. Fifteen times a night, and no sleep in between. In the jail I was really able to sleep and relax. Then Paula came to visit me and told me how things stood. Everything would have been okay but out of the kindness of my heart I'd left all the booze in the trunk of the Mercedes, and the guy had opened it and realized there was a whole liquor store included in the deal. He hadn't spent any time thinking about it, just called the cops and told them that someone had filled the trunk of his car with booze during the night. He'd had a terrible hangover and really didn't feel like any more booze that morning, I guess. My fingerprints were everywhere, and Paula's too. They let themselves into Paula's with their own keys. She was in bed, still stark naked of course, when the cops came in. They got her purse and soon figured out our weekend route. The last flight from Joensuu to Helsinki. So that was our weekend. Paula let me fuck her in the ass when she visited, so I don't see any reason for being depressed. We've agreed that we'll do it all again as soon as I get out.

THE LIGHT FROM THE LAMP ON THE NIGHT TABLE FELL OBLIQUELY on the double bed. The woman lay in the middle of the bed, fat and naked. The man put his empty beer bottle on the floor and flopped on top of her. She slid slowly away from him, muttering to herself something he couldn't make out. He rolled over on his back and glanced at her belly, which was covered in old folds of fat.

"How do you want it?"

The woman was silent and didn't move for a long time.

"I could sit on top of you."

"Wouldn't work," he said, and turned his back.

The woman lit a cigarette, took three drags, and put it in the ashtray. The red cigarette end glowed in the semi-darkness of the room.

"Forget it, then," she said, and closed her eyes.

"How about if I tried from the side," the man said in a bleating voice.

The woman turned her head and looked with disgust at his fat, pimply back.

"Wouldn't be any good," she said, and pulled the blanket over her.

The man turned round, sank his hand deep into the fat at the woman's waist, pulled her towards him and whispered.

"From behind, the usual way."

The woman smiled, stubbed out the dead cigarette end in the ashtray, and positioned her enormous backside at a suitable height in front of him.

IT WAS EARLY SUMMER AND THERE WAS STILL SO MUCH TO DO.
The sacks of artificial fertilizer stood in a heap at the end of the
cowshed and the rain was making holes in them and spreading
the saltpeter into the ground where it got hard as stone. All the
fertilizer was going to waste since my husband couldn't manage to fix the seeding machine behind the tractor and drive it
out to the field. He'd started drinking at the beginning of May
and had kept it up for nearly two months. Everything still
needed to be done, and I was working like crazy, repairing the
fence-posts, putting up new electric fencing, planting potatoes, everything. The worst of it was that he didn't drink with
the other men in the village, but here at home. When I did the
milking, he sat on a potato crate yapping away about this and
that as I went by, and when I was baking he stood at my shoulder slobbering. I told him several times in no uncertain words
that he'd have to stop drinking, otherwise it would all end

badly, but it didn't go any good. He just shouted that the man of the house got to say what was what. Shouting was all he did, he never raised a hand to me, but kept barking on and on about his great achievements, which were just a lot of bullshit. I decided that I wasn't going to go on living like that until the grave. Well, I'm the kind of woman who won't just let herself be thrown around like a sack of flour. I told him it was over now. My husband laughed and told me to shut up, but I took the hunting rifle down from the wall and fired one shot and he was dead. There he lay, didn't even give so much as a wriggle. There was blood all over the place, and I wondered which I should do first, start cleaning up or call the chief of police. I cleaned up first, since you don't invite an important person over when the place is like a pigsty. I went and fetched several buckets of water from the cowshed and cleaned it all up. I had to think of my boys, too, since if they came back from the lake and saw that bloodbath they wouldn't exactly be pleased. I washed and scrubbed, and threw the dirty water on the trash heap, so it wouldn't get mixed up with the water from the well. When it was all cleaned up, I wiped the worst of the bloodstains off my husband and took off his sweater, since there was blood all over it. Then I put the rifle by the door and called the police. I said the police chief should bring the hearse, since there was a body in the parlor. They immediately asked whose body it was. I said it was my husband's. They didn't ask any more questions, just asked me to wait calmly. "Wait," can you imagine? It was already three o' clock and I had to start making dinner for the boys. I put the pork bones on to cook; I'd already set the peas to soak at five that morning. I made the meal and washed the breakfast bowls out since it was the chief of police himself who was coming, and I got some pastries out of the freezer so they'd have time to thaw. When the boys came home, the eldest appeared first and stood there in the doorway.

"What the hell is that lying there?" he asked.

I said that our poor bull had gone and died at last. The boy nodded and looked relieved; he stepped over the body and sat down to eat. He was very hungry after being out on the lake all day. The younger one came next, and he didn't ask any questions, probably thought his father had passed out on the floor as usual. We ate, and then washed the dishes again, set the table for the police chief, went out and watered the calves, and put out hay for the cows. It was evening when the police chief arrived together with a constable, and of course they hadn't brought the hearse with them. I asked where we were going to put the body if there wasn't a hearse. They said there was enough room in the back of their car even for a big man. The boys stayed in their room and watched TV, and I served coffee and buns. They asked about the seeding, and I explained that the seeding should have been done almost two months ago, but there was no man in the house to do it. Then I got on with packing a suitcase and was thinking of sending the boys to their granny, when the police followed me into the bedroom and said there was no need to pack anything, that they would take care of everything. I was really pleased that I wouldn't have to send the boys to their granny, and that there was no need to order a truck to take the cows away. I served them a third cup of coffee and felt strangely content.

"If only I could just find a decent man," I said.

The police chief went out to the car and fetched a big black bag. They put the body in it and hauled it back to the car. All I heard was a bump. The boys didn't come out to look, there was a good program on TV just then. When I was outside I asked the police if they wanted me to bring the rifle with me, but they didn't. A week later we held the funeral, my husband was put in the ground, and no one asked any more about it. In the first week of July the boys and I got on with the haymaking, though there wasn't much this year, since the fertilizer stayed in the sacks unused.

SELECTED DALKEY ARCHIVE PAPERBACKS

SELECTED DALKEY ARCHIVE PAPERBACKS

FOR A FULL LIST OF PUBLICATIONS, VISIT: WWW.DALKEYARCHIVE.COM